Little Ducks Go

by Emily Arnold McCully

Holiday House / New York

I Like to Read®

Library of Congress Cataloging-in-Publication Data
McCully, Emily Arnold, author, illustrator.
Little ducks go / by Emily Arnold McCully. — First edition.
pages cm. — (I like to read)
Summary: Mother Duck is on the run trying
to keep her ducklings safe.
ISBN 978-0-8234-2941-7 (hardcover)
[1. Ducks—Fiction.
2. Animals—Infancy—Fiction.]
I. Title.
PZ7.M478415Lhm 2014
[E]—dc23
2013009559

Little ducks go.

Look out, little ducks!

Little ducks go.

They go down.

Mother looks down.

"Quack," she says.

Little ducks look up.

"Cheep cheep," they say.

Little ducks go.

Mother runs.

Mother looks down.

"Quack!"

Little ducks look up.

"Cheep cheep!"

Little ducks go.

Mother runs.

Cars come.

Look out!

She is safe.

Mother runs.

Little ducks go.

"Cheep cheep!"

Little ducks stop.

Mother stops too.

She wants help.

But the man goes away.

Mother looks down.

"Quack," she says.

"Cheep cheep," she hears.

She sits.

The man comes back.

Little ducks get into the net.

They are safe!

Little ducks go home.
"Cheep cheep cheep
cheep cheep cheep!"
"Quack!"

You will like these too!

The Big Fib by Tim Hamilton

Dinosaurs Don't, Dinosaurs Do
by Steve Björkman

Fish Had a Wish by Michael Garland
Kirkus Reviews Best Children's Books list
and Top 25 Children's Books list

I Said, "Bed!" by Bruce Degen

I Will Try by Marilyn Janovitz

Look! by Ted Lewin

Pete Won't Eat by Emily Arnold McCully

See Me Run by Paul Meisel
A Theodor Seuss Geisel Award Honor Book

See more I Like to Read books.
Go to www.holidayhouse.com/I-Like-to-Read/